This book is

WANTED

and belongs to

. . . .

For
Francesca and Pui
Love D

For Laura,
who looks cute
when she wears a cowgirl suit
JE

First
published in
Great Britain in 2006
by Egmont UK Limited
239 Kensington High Street,
London W8 6SA

Text copyright © Jonathan Emmett 2006
Illustrations copyright © Deborah Allwright 2006
The author and illustrator have asserted their moral rights
A CIP catalogue for this title is available from The British Library

ISBN 10 - 1 4052 2649 8 (Hardback)   ISBN 13 - 978 1 4052 2649 3 (Hardback)
ISBN 10 - 1 4052 2650 1 (Paperback)   ISBN 13 - 978 1 4052 2650 9 (Paperback)

Colour reproduction by Dot Gradations Ltd, UK   Printed in Italy
10 9 8 7 6 5 4 3 2   All rights reserved.

You can find out more about Jonathan Emmett's books
by visiting his website at www.scribblestreet.co.uk

She'll
BE COMING
Round the
MOUNTAIN

Jonathan Emmett   **Deborah Allwright**

EGMONT

Gather round now!
I'm gonna tell y'all about a special visitor . . .

She'll be coming round the mountain when she comes,

Toot-Toot!

She'll be coming round the mountain when she comes,

Toot-Toot!

Yes, she'll whistle like a train,
As she speeds across the plain,
She'll be coming round the mountain
when she comes,

Toot-Toot!

She'll be driving six white horses when she comes,

WHOA BACK!

She'll be driving six white horses when she comes,

WHOA BACK!

They're called Misty, Moonbeam, Milkshake,
Stardust, Silvermane and Snowflake,
She'll be driving six white horses
when she comes,

WHOA BACK!
Toot-Toot!

She'll be wearing
pink pyjamas when she comes,

Tee - Hee!

She'll be wearing pink pyjamas
when she comes,

Tee - Hee!

They are flowery and frilly,
And they make her look quite silly,
She'll be wearing pink pyjamas when she comes,

Tee - Hee!

WHOA BACK!

Toot - Toot!

She'll be juggling with jelly when she comes,
Squish-Splat!

She'll be juggling with jelly when she comes,
Squish-Splat!

If you ask her as a favour,
She will let you choose the flavour!
She'll be juggling with jelly when she comes,

Squish-Splat!

Tee-Hee!

WHOA BACK!

Toot-Toot!

And she'll dance across the rooftops when she comes,
Yee-Ha!
Yes, she'll dance across the rooftops when she comes,
Yee-Ha!

And you won't believe how nimbly
She can boogie round the **chimbly**,

Yes, she'll dance across the rooftops when she comes,

Yee-Ha! Squish-Splat! Tee-Hee! WHOA BACK! Toot-Toot!

And she'll paint the whole town purple when she comes,
Bish-Bosh!
Yes, she'll paint the whole town purple when she comes,
Bish-Bosh!

And the place won't
look so glum,
When it's coloured
like a plum,

Yes, she'll paint the whole town purple when she comes,

Bish-Bosh!

Yee-Ha!

Squish-Splat!

Tee-Hee!

WHOA BACK!

Toot-Toot!

And she'll drink out of a dustbin when she comes,

SLURP-SLURP!

Yes, she'll drink out of a dustbin when she comes,

SLURP-SLURP!

Unless it's ginger ale,
Which she drinks out of a pail,

Yes, she'll drink out of a dustbin when she comes,

SLURP-SLURP!

Bish-Bosh!

Yee-Ha!

Squish-Splat!

Tee-Hee!

WHOA BACK!

Toot-Toot!

And we'll all go out to meet her when she comes,
HI BABE!

And we'll all go out to meet her when she comes,

HI BABE!

So I hope that you are clear
On what to say when she gets here!

Because she's coming round the mountain . . .

HI BABE!

SLURP-SLURP!

Bish-Bosh!

Yee-Ha!

Here she

comes!

Squish-Splat!

Tee-Hee!

WHOA BACK!

Toot-Toot!

Well I guess someone must have told y'all that I was comin'!

Toot-Toot!

Pull on the chain of a steam whistle

WHOA BACK!

Pull back on the horse's reins with both hands

Tee - Hee!

Cover your mouth with your hands

Squish-Splat!

Juggle the jelly with both hands

Why don't y'all read the book again —

Yee-Ha!

Swing a lassoo
above your head

Bish-Bosh!

Paint with big up
and down strokes

**SLURP-
SLURP!**

Lean back, grip the
dustbin and drink

HI BABE!

Give a big
wave hello

but this time doing these actions with each of the sounds?